Published by The Child's World®
1980 Lookout Drive • Mankato, MN 56003-1705
800-599-READ • www.childsworld.com

ACKNOWLEDGMENTS
The Child's World®: Mary Berendes, Publishing Director
The Design Lab: Kathleen Petelinsek, Design and Page Production
Literacy Consultants: Cecilia Minden, PhD, and Joanne Meier, PhD

LIBRARY OF CONGRESS
CATALOGING-IN-PUBLICATION DATA
Moncure, Jane Belk.
  My "v" sound box / by Jane Belk Moncure ;
illustrated by Rebecca Thornburgh.
    p. cm. — (Sound box books)
  Summary: "Little v has an adventure with items beginning
with her letter's sound, such as violets, a veil, and lots of velvet
valentines."—Provided by publisher.
  ISBN 978-1-60253-162-8 (library bound : alk. paper)
  [1. Alphabet.] I. Thornburgh, Rebecca McKillip, ill. II. Title.
III. Series.
  PZ7.M739Myv 2009
  [E]–dc22   2008033178

Printed in the United States of America • Mankato, MN
August, 2011 • PA02105

A NOTE TO PARENTS AND EDUCATORS:

Magic moon machines and five fat frogs are just a few of the fun things you can share with children by reading books with them. Reading aloud helps children in so many ways! It introduces them to new words, motivates them to develop their own reading skills, and expands their attention span and listening abilities. So it's important to find time each day to share a book or two . . . or three!

As you read with young children, you can help develop their understanding of how print works by talking about the parts of the book—the cover, the title, the illustrations, and the words that tell the story. As you read, use your finger to point to each word, modeling a gentle sweep from left to right.

Simple word games help develop important prereading skills, including an understanding of rhyme and alliteration (when words share the same beginning sound, such as "six" and "sand"). Try playing with words from a book you've just shared: "What other words start with the same sound as moon?" "Cat and hat, do those words rhyme?" The possibilities are endless—and so are the rewards!

Roses are
red,
Violets are
blue,
Sugar is sweet,
So are you!

My "v" Sound Box®

To
my
friend

VINE
CIDE

WRITTEN BY JANE BELK MONCURE

ILLUSTRATED BY REBECCA THORNBURGH

Little  had a box. "I will

find things that begin with my

V sound," she said. "I will put

them into my sound box."

Little  found violets, all kinds

of pretty violets.

She put some violets into a vase.

Then she put the vase with the

violets into her box.

Next, Little  found a piece of velvet, very pretty velvet.

She made a velvet vest. She put it

on and pinned a velvet bow on it.

She put velvet all around her box.

 "What a very pretty box," she said.

Little  found a veil.

"Oh," she said. "I can make

something with my violets and

velvet and veil."

Do you know what Little  made? She made valentines,
very nice valentines.

Then she found a valentine verse.

Roses are red.

Violets are blue.

Sugar is sweet.

So are you!

She wrote the verse on her valentines.

Then she filled her box with 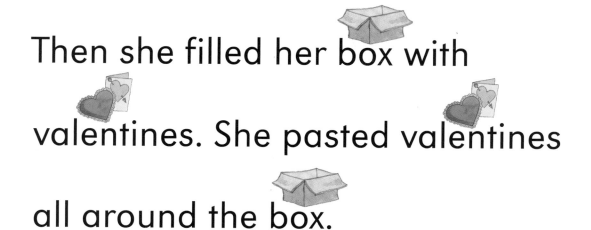 valentines. She pasted valentines all around the box.

But some valentines fell out.

"What shall I do with all these

valentines?" she said.

"I will send the valentines to my friends." Then Little  had a very good idea.

She wrote another verse on

each valentine.

Come to my party at one, for Valentine's Day fun.

She put the valentines into
envelopes. She put her friends'
names and addresses on the
envelopes. There were very many.

Little 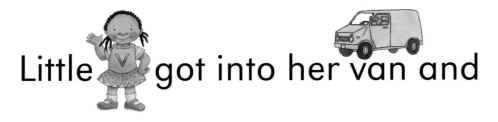 got into her van and

drove to the mailbox.

When Little  got back home,

she got out the vacuum.

She used the vacuum to clean up

the scraps of velvet and valentines.

On Valentine's Day, her friends

came to her party. Each one

brought valentines.

Little  and her friends made

valentine hats.

They put on their valentine hats

and played some games.

Then they opened the valentines.

What fun they had at the

Valentine's Day party!

Little 's Word List

vacuum

vase

verse

valentines

veil

vest

van

velvet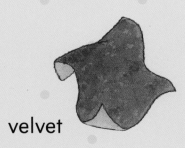

violet

Other Words with Little

valley

vine

vitamins

vampire

vinegar

volcano

vegetables

violin

volleyball

More to Do!

 Little had fun making valentines for her friends. They were celebrating Valentine's Day, which is on February 14. But you don't need to wait until Valentine's Day to make special cards for special people. You can make them right now!

What you need:

- construction paper or card stock
- crayons
- markers
- sequins, stickers, and glitter for decorating
- glue

Directions:

1. Fold the piece of paper in half.

2. Decorate the front of the card with a nice picture or design. Some fun  **V** things you could draw include violets in a vase, your favorite vegetables, or flowers on a vine. Use the other materials you have to make a beautiful card.

3. Then write a nice verse on the inside. Write your name and seal it with a kiss!

About the Author

Best-selling author Jane Belk Moncure has written over 300 books throughout her teaching and writing career. After earning a Master's degree in Early Childhood Education from Columbia University, she became one of the pioneers in that field. In 1956, she helped form the Virginia Association for Early Childhood Education, which established the first statewide standards for teachers of young children.

Inspired by her work in the classroom, Mrs. Moncure's books have become standards in primary education, and her name is recognized across the country. Her success is reflected not only in her books' popularity with parents, children, and educators, but also by numerous awards, including the 1984 C. S. Lewis Gold Medal Award.

About the Illustrator

Rebecca Thornburgh lives in a pleasantly spooky old house in Philadelphia. If she's not at her drawing table, she's reading—or singing with her band, called Reckless Amateurs. Rebecca has one husband, two daughters, and two silly dogs.